Nixes Mate Anthology
In the Time of Covid

EDITED BY CONSTELLATION FUNKHOUSER,

MICHAEL MCINNIS + ANNIE PLUTO

Nixes Mate Books
Allston, Massachusetts

ISBN 978-1-949279-39-9

Nixes Mate Books
POBox 1179
Allston, MA 02134
nixesmate.pub

And so when Master Codington saide, What do you Dutch call that,
Dirke saide "Nixie Schmalt," I do not know how to spell it, but it
meaneth the Wail of the Water Spirit, or the Water Spirit is chiding.
But Master Codington thought it was the name of the Iland, and set
it down on the map he had Nix his Mate Island.
— Rich Burbeck, as quoted by Moses Sweetser in his *Handbook.*

CONTENTS

Nixes Mate Anthology

In the Time of Covid

TRAVELIN' LIGHT **JONATHAN PENTON**

Alison Saar
American, born 1956
Travelin' Light, 1999
Bronze
Gift from the family and friends of Sunny Norman on
the occasion of her 90th birthday, 2001.248
Installation funded by Mrs. P. Roussel Norman

My Black wife and I went to a gallery opening. The exhibit was a mix of painted photographs and mixed-media sculptures on the subject of the lynching of Black Southerners. The artist was a white man, and he was attempting to explain his work to two other white men, as well as educate them on the source material and events. The two observers were agitated and aroused, thrilled to be there, opening night, for such an important exhibit. They said that the subject was painfully heavy, but they found it cathartic, as well. My wife did not sleep that night.

This sculpture is a man hanging from a rope.
He is upside-down.   He is hanging from his feet.
His head is hollow.   His head is a bell.

The clapper had to be removed from his skull so that people would stop ringing it.
That is what I know.

My first job in a sandwich shop
the saloon doors plastered
with the two halves of Farrah.
Red swimsuit, a Mexican blanket,
those nipples. I'd bust through
her and place the orders for veal
Parmigiana or a large American,

hots or no hots
pepper and egg on Friday, the Catholic
owner's specialty. He'd make each sub
handing it out, holding back Farrah's
shoulder. Each night the aluminum
stock pot of sausages was put under foil
the top oily, red and dark, a good
burn worked into the sauce.

I could put an Italian to bed, the soft
padding of the roll, a pillow of white
bread, sheets of mortadella and salami

rose medallions of marbled fat
three slices each, angels themselves,
then good provolone, that barely wants to
bend. I'd tuck in tomatoes and pickles,
then oil, a sprinkle of salt and pepper
already mixed together. If you had done it right
it wouldn't want to close.

AT ONCE **YVONNE HIGGINS LEACH**

North of the peninsula
we can see for miles on both sides:
barns, farmhouses, and how the deep
measure of light
tongues the tall grass.

The North Atlantic wind
beats into our faces.
Sea arches, salt spray, the smell of peat.
Sometimes I wish for better days,
but not today.

You slow the car –
what was vast is now singular.
A tribunal of cows saunters
across the road
from one field to another.

Heads hang like lanterns,
a chorus of hooves,
jabbing of shoulder blades.
This procession of trust knows
no timetable.

Be it the sweet prod
of the farmer's voice
or all of us watching
in silence,
we are home.

Today is pleasurably mute, infused with the stillness of the man-swarm. There pervades a comforting lack of voices on a late Sunday afternoon. That point outside when darkness clings to the last strain of light before succumbing to its inevitable aloneness. Bracing itself for that shudder of solitude. Its lonely plight is without fail. The waning hours paint themselves more dismally on this day when streets call out to take refuge in their blank, silent embrace. Maybe a chorus of a million mute cries bank off the muddy puddles, endless rain taps against the panes that stare out with a frightened eye and wonder what it is they must do.

Numberless cold plates sit on tabletops, scatter remains of potatoes, carrots. Endless hands hold forks in bleary kitchens as eyes stare out of icebox windows into other darkened windows. Row after row, street after street, single lit rooms trail one another until each blurs into the next, yet somehow exist apart.

A travesty of foggy dreams splay out into the damp atmosphere, multiply through the soot-ridden avenues. Anyway who dares to walk these sidewalks spirals into cacklings of empty hope. Pedestrians glut with aches of fixations–an invisible collusion links the melancholy plight like holding hands with the ruinous multitude, as though one's own weight wasn't enough.

Rain, winds rise like sounds of Mahler. The winding trances of woodwinds. Battling wail of flutes. Lurk of the brass surrounds.

The sinking doom of another Monday imprisons us with its rattling monotony; its migraine pace. The conspiratorial rasp of the clock snickers and the numb tread of men loop the same track with impunity.

I sit in my kitchen, fork dangling in my fingers. I look out into the dim light of a kitchen with another hunched figure who leans over his plate, who stares out a window at yet another figure. We watch for the creep of hours like the face of another life.

AFTER HER THIRD WEDDING THIS SUMMER MY THIRTY-YEAR-OLD DAUGHTER IS WONDERING **SARAH DICKENSON SNYDER**

Is she asking too much
of the men she meets –
not to fly a plane

or jump between
sky scrapers, but perhaps
like that – to leap from this to that,

to peel back
layers to the rush
of gravity.

MOTTLED **SUSAN TEPPER**

After exile you plant
fire in the garden
the soil seeded
deep rows
yields a mottled leaf:
one to shade the yard
eventually another
becomes the sea
in autumn –
early sunset blazing
makes your forget summer
the table's red cloth
stained from the morning coffee –
you wanted to be happy
but forgot
the sun rise over purple clouds
drifting, a sky
that pulses your veins
once forced currents

an undertow that pulled
your ankles to knots
– then forgetting, looked back.

I prefer your light stomped underground –
smothered and sucking what drips
from the sweet water of my saccharine nod
doled to mollify my thousandth savage barb.
I'm composed of eye roll and ear steam,
putrid green. The stakes are low, and all mine
unless I deign to launch one into your chest
for daring to be third party to my party.
No. I won't admit you. You're a sorry oaf
for caring. I'm born of wire monkey and glib
need to devour, empowered at the helm
of my stingy verse realm where I'm Queen Bee.
A hex on you for your sin of seeing me.

Eventually you will turn yourself in
after a long day of fishing and the cat

dead as a brick thrown through
your parlor window. What light?

Did you expect to look up
and see golden shields? Instead

you woke in a ship in a field
of black roses with one arm in

and one arm out, forced to trace
a blank map with cloudy eyes.

You'll remember something about
bowling, something about a wrap-

around porch and hearing
your name. I wonder why it is

we say *riddled* when we're talking about
death? What is there to figure?

The chosen are no better off than
the unchosen. Study it from different angles

it's always death. You can balance
a soap bubble on your finger, turn

a feather and see such luminous colors.
Iris as the seashell's intimate curl, under-

belly of the mackerel you put on ice.
You can't help playing devil's advocate even

while you're sipping tea with your
father and his cancer and your mother

watching you worriedly
from across the room.

BURNT TOAST **ARIANNA SEBO**

She asked me what was up with my
spice cupboard
the paprika was mixed in with the
lemon pepper and the cinnamon with
the honey
I told her I don't supervise my
cupboards after hours
I do have a roommate who often
comes home in the wee hours of the
morning, though
Sometimes I hear him crisping
strange things on my George Foreman
grill
I wish he would quit burning
my toast

OXY **LINDA LAMENZA**

I've been awake since the day
I met your incessant silence,
me with deafening dreams.

You are fickle.
So often you go missing.
And always, I collapse with joy
at your return.

Entangled in the line,
I take the bait,
follow your lead, but never get it right.

We haven't had rain in twelve days, and the grass is
August-brown in late June.
Cue the marching lines of fire ants.
Blessed are the meek, I guess,
for they shall inherit the next great flood.

It is not for us to question. Scientists and engineers didn't
build the ark. On my way to the bike shop I saw
a sign on an embattled front lawn: God. Guns.
Country. (There were no bikes.)
The Arctic just topped 100 degrees,
prelude to the lake of fire.

You have to give it to Him: He speaks His mind.
There are brown caterpillars in Maine whose tiny hairs
get into your clothes causing an all-body itch, distressed
breathing. We keep reading that children are carriers.
Hose everything down. Those hairs float in dry air,
don't even dry your clothes in the sun.

Taking to the streets is the new minivan.
Teenagers swap selfies for signs, face shields, humanity itself.
My son, disgusted that we don't fish,
made his own rig out of a stick and grey yarn.
He's gotten a few bites.
The Lord works in mysterious ways.

(After Hopkins)

It's not about you anymore,
hope, my cardinal sin.

I've run out of recall and no one else's sharing their stories
and that leaves me in the middle
of this trestle bridge,
staring off, smarting still
from your cursed crimson flight
across frozen water, where blown snows streak,
squiggling closest to ghost.

The therapists insisted you were a must,
had to keep you on the wing, going the distance,
those guardrailed miles between institutions
until he would just outgrow this,
like ear infections or bedwetting.

Your bright-blooded flutter
made me look the other way,
saying, "Someday, he'll go back to school. Find himself,"
when he cried in the shower.

Hope kept the glass half full,
a needed drink after steering him through
lunch and a movie on the half-day pass.

Hope kept me humoring him along,
like any other kid who eventually declares, "You know I never
        asked to be born!"

Only he added, "Please, Mom, respect my choice
to leave the world.
I was given none to enter it.
Love, your son."

I LOST A SMALL FOREST **KENNETH POBO**

Owls went with it
and many ferns.
I knew some owls
by name.

A cinnamon fern
grew by a creek.
We didn't talk.
I waved
as I walked by.

Clear cutters
killed off
much of it.

I can still walk
around there –
waiting for birds
that never come.

in memory of my mother

One day a hundred and two years ago my mother stood
by her own mother's casket.
It was the time of the Spanish Flu.
Four years old, she asked the maid who held her hand:
Who will now give us our bread?
Did the young woman fold her gently into her arms?
Did she say: *We will. We'll do our best.*

Twenty-seven years later she stood in line at a mill,
two hungry sons and a hungry sister waiting
back at their makeshift refugee home. She had no grain
to trade for bread like farmers did. She had nothing
except the humility to beg. The miller, reading her
thin situation didn't make her beg, but gruffly asked:
And how many do you get? Pedaling home
on a borrowed bicycle with two loaves,
it was a happy day for her.

She was always a lady, *hlaf-dige*, giver of bread.

Give us this day our daily bread, we pray
and then forget to value the familiar. It is raining
and the air smells of yeast and spice. I remember
the world through her eyes: stockings with lace
embroidery down the side, delicate dresses,
and bold Sunday hats. She served me bread with honey
and hot chocolate on winter mornings.
Winter is always a good time to remember who I am.
Spring, too. I am still hungry. Still curious
about her many secrets. The men in her life treated her
like some kind of furniture, a sturdy convenience.
Too soon she died from destiny and complications
of unhappiness. I am her hungry daughter.
Who will give us our bread?

The bread in my freezer will last a while,
even in these fragile times. I keep dreaming
this time it will be different. This time breadcrumbs
will show me the way back home. Home
has become unfamiliar so quickly.

~~FEELING~~ BURYING HER PAIN

After Gwendolyn Brooks' "A Sunset of the City"

I worried all night until I
could not fret any more. I am
tired – tired of losing sleep to a
man who does not know I am a woman;
therefore, I bury my pain more than those who
are open and free. I am the one who hurries
through my sorrow, who does not want to go through
pain, because then I am weak; the one who doesn't see her-
self as others do. The one who saves those tears for her prayers.

I'm trying to hold on to the sunset over the lighthouse at the edge
of the Cape but the tornadoes we drove home through threaten
to erase it from my mind. We never reached the lighthouse. The
white-headed dog got sunstroke and collapsed in the sand. We
hitched a ride back to the bed & breakfast. Now, the people who
know me best have never met me. The few I love, I hold in my
fist like the wooden tulips I bought myself one Mother's Day. The
news inserts itself into my sleep—the faces of judges who should
not be, the children still in cages. I used to read, incredulous,
about the crimes of the past. Now that we have our own concen-
tration camps and ghettos, I am finished with history.

Sontag wrote, "Someone who is permanently surprised that
depravity exists…when confronted with evidence of what humans
are capable of inflicting in the way of gruesome, hands-on cruel-
ties upon other humans, has not reached moral or psychological
adulthood." One fall, not long ago, I grew up. The pumpkins,
piled in cardboard boxes pitied me as I walked past. I used to hold
my tongue like the good girl I was taught to be, hair brushed and

braided. The waves beat the whale-watching boat but the tide was there for me, returning me to the months I was pregnant and told I could not end it. By my husband. By my mother. Today, a woman has voted against all women. I am not surprised.

Sontag was right. "It hurts to love. It's like giving yourself to be flayed and knowing that at any moment the other person may just walk off with your skin." I am safe on the cold beach picking shells. Every child on the sand knows this dilemma. The shells all look perfect, cradled in the wet sand, before you bend and hold them, find each dull and dry in your hands. I stash a few in a chocolate tin with a watercolor of the lighthouse on the lid. They sit on a small cake plate of hot pink depression glass. I touch the tiny matching shells that feel like mother-of pearl. I memorize the one I found so I know which one is mine.

Sometimes on Sundays
I hide under the cathedral's altar
the gold-embroidered white linen
framing a perfect secret lair,
while the priest murmurs Mass
above me, in the cold incantations
of ancient Latin. I can feel
the weight of 2,000 years of death,
flagellation, and resurrection
emanating from the cross downward
toward me to shelter my sins,
outward toward the congregation
beckoning them to understand,
and upward toward heaven
where it receives ultimate release!
They all sit quietly reciting prayers
they don't comprehend,
while I pray God will spare me
the priest's marauding hands

at least on this holy day,
that he will leave me, for once,
in peace. I pray under the altar
until my body emerges
to perform its Eucharistic duty,
to transmogrify as it is consumed.
May God have mercy on my soul.

Time was on the table –
sun, sensual in a November way.
I was standing, pondering, a horse before space.

. . .

At Sea
All is beautiful,
terror has eyes of stars.

. . .

Stunning fall, fiery brown,
reigns again.
I have nerve – I return its gaze.

SOME SWEET CATHERINE ARRA

You came around at dusk, alone
ears tuned toward woods for the rustle
or mew of your new offspring.

Attentive mother, fatigued after fawning, you wanted
the bundle of apple pieces all at once, not our usual
one-by-one toss & talk.

I chatted away through each crunch-saliva-slipping chew
& long-neck swallow – asked you how it went, the birthing.
How many this year, one or two?

How tired you must be from cleaning, concealing, suckling
& how many fawns before? Five that I know of.
Now six, seven?

I told you how Leaf, your yearling boy, came around
this morning; what a fine sturdy-legged buck he is;
what a good mother you are.

I told you my prayer for you to live long in green peace,
to never suffer or perish by human hands, to die sleeping
in a quilted-leaf bed under your favorite tree & best-loved breeze.

You swallowed the last apple wedge & stepped to me,
a full-body-neck-stretch, closer than you have ever … I stilled,
matched instincts, & for a moment we were timeless,

a bare breath apart
like Michelangelo's almost touch
of God & man.

I felt you whisper, more …
more sweet crunch, more sweet after strain,
more sweetness, please.

I scurried into the house,
quickly sliced another, this time in a pan of corn too
& placed all before you.

You will do this year after year
until you no longer can, or die. What compels you
through the cycles & seasonal trials –

the rigors of rut, the race against hunters' guns
the hollow hunger in winter
to do it over & over

& still look into me with wild-doe love?

1. (R)egrets

My poems have too many birds; it's like that damn Hitchcock movie in here. Lots of them are sparrows, because you're supposed to write what you know and sparrows are all over this city. The rest of the birds I don't dare specify. People are always putting birds they've never seen in poems, like albatrosses and phoenixes and doves. I don't trust them. They're just abstractions in bird suits.

2. Floriography

I won't name a flower in a poem either. In junior high, the student council sold carnations for Valentine's Day. You had to know the code: pink for friendship, white for admiration, red for love. Blundering, I sent a red one to my best friend, and for months savvier girls followed us around hissing *lesbians*. That was before I realized that they were probably right, about me at least. Poems are like junior high that way.

3. Deciduous

Trees are even worse, because they all look the same to me. Once I signed up to be apprenticed to a naturalist for the summer and learn what everything is called. He wore a necklace made of his own baby teeth. I lived in a cabin in the woods where he tried to convince me he was God. I wanted to be susceptible to this, but it didn't work out. The fact is, no one knows which kind of tree is which. They are all just making it up.

TRAIL OF ROOTS **GAIL THOMAS**

Maybe I must forget what I thought
I knew about walking to hike this trail

with my dog who is thrilled to be free.
This is not a time for ambling, not *Shinrin Yoku*,

forest bathing, where one walks untethered.
Though slice of sky beyond the canopy

stares like the milky blue eye of a newborn,
today my eyes only focus on feet, what lies

beneath and ahead. Tangled web of roots
course like bruised veins at every angle,

matted leaves layered with a thousand years
of dead news lined with scarlet mushrooms,

waist high wings of ferns. In China children
wear brightly painted butterfly wings to keep

six feet of distance in school. What bird is making
that sawing noise, or is it a porcupine high in an oak

ready to drop a gnawed branch for its young?
The years when I used my body and skin to feed

my children, denied by their father, a blind
alley with stacks of bills and ragged clothes.

Follow the blue blaze on the next tree, lift
a low hanging branch before it slaps my face,

then an uphill stretch and downhill tumble of pebbles,
more up and down until calves and toes cramp, and I

begin to stumble. Pushing a stroller, walking home
from a pride march, holding my other child's hand,

red faced men screamed at us. In our garden, a teenage
neighbor spit on the ground, the thick clot daring

me to protect them. And now a bridge
of wet boards spread across shallow muck, where

the dog's desire to tramp in black sludge is met.
Orange newt skitters across a decaying stump,

home for larvae and beetles. Sweating, I tear
a wide frond of fern to swat the gnats that swarm

like bullies who taunted on the school bus,
You're dykes just like your mother.

The lovers who came and left, distraction and guilt
like borers leave sawdust around my heart.

Blocking the path, a storm struck white pine
stretches out like a corpse. I hoist myself

over its rough bulk, balance then straddle
before lowering to solid ground. Flecks

of pine wings rain down, souls of dark skinned
boys, child soldiers, girl brides, babies lost

at the border, unmasked and innocent.
The bounding dog comes back to check

then runs ahead again, nose to the ground
on the scent of something I cannot see.

Foot against white-painted steel, I look up,
the sky an eggshell of light, the boats all fiberglass finery
moored in the harbor beneath a building raised
stone by stone in 1708 – granite blocks
and iron balconies,
            where Elizabeth Bishop might have lived
with her lover, a slight girl in a button-down Oxford
and black capris. Decades ago, in the last century.

The breeze pushes humid air into something finer
and a young girl in a purple shirt that reads
girl power (n) – the idea of a young girl
being strong and powerful
bends and unbends against the railing.

The boat hoots and slides glass-like from the dock,
past wide, white windows ramshackle on their pilings.
The girl's voice rises from the stir of conversation, then a man's.
Sharp-dark smell of the boat's diesel engine,
all the buildings of the North End slant past:

brick walls and leaded glass, mansard roofs and slanted roofs.
In the distance, the Tobin Bridge swoops twice at its highest points,
greened copper, and then the boat turns,
presents the cluster of tall buildings at the waterfront,
their shiny glass, the clock tower of the Customs House,
crown of downtown with its ghosts
of old rebellions, slaves and merchant ships,
the golden lion and the unicorn on the old State House
with a subway in its basement.

We pass Fort Point Channel, and the glass wall
of the Federal Courthouse slants above us—
the ferry tour guide says it's meant to be
like a tidal wave of justice over the harbor.
Derricks rise over steel skeletons – the city's
always building on itself. I search for what's left
of the piers
      where the No Name restaurant
still serves corn and cod, the ghost of the Channel
nightclub where water lapped beneath cracks in the floorboards
and a solid wall of sound

rose gritty and loud above the mosh-pit –
                                        decades ago,
in the last century. Now all gone to condos, bamboo floors,
in-unit washer-dryers, anomie, dyspepsia.

Bright crowds line the quay beneath the ICA.
The boat cuts over sparkles, makes a shush that overlays
the babble of voices all around us,
thrum of the engine, while the sun burns my toes
where I've braced them on the railing,
and a container ship with *Yang Ming*
inscribed in yellow on its side sports
Lego-block containers full of stereos
and teddy bears from China,
and Castle Island slides past, its earthworks and turf roofs.
Tiny people promenade between the water
and the sunburned grass, and in the distance
the Great Blue Hills lump along
                                        with the ghosts
of the Massachusett who named them, the ghosts
of the English who stole them.

The boat roils and rumbles, slowing as it reaches
an island made of two round hills
joined by a spit of land to look like spectacles,
an island that housed a glue factory
                              and then a garbage dump,
and now has green drumlins studded with cottonwood trees
that rustle in the hot July breeze, and there's
a jazz trio on Sundays at the pier, and a snack bar
serving beer and sandwiches, and a bath-house,
and a tiny pebbled beach, and my own round body
bobbing in the waves, with the Boston skyline
orienting me home, over the harbor.

I can taste this image. The way his grin
splits his face apart leaves a whiff
of adrenaline and another scent

I can't quite place but want to crawl inside
each time it pheromones from him to me.
This grin splits me apart with a sharp

craving to lap the glee into my cracked
lips. If I were this grinning boy
I wouldn't have been the girl who fell

down a rabbit hole chasing long-eared
shadows. Perhaps my teeth would show
like a wolf's, panting after the hunt.

I dream, too. In this dream, Judy's rage ruffles the quiet cut-outs of her collar. *Madame!* she shouts at the teen mother whose boyfriend's Pitbull bites. First it was the boyfriend and his infected tattoo. Then his five kids. Then the biting dog. My mother's telling Judy about her girlhood mutt, Shadow, a dark cannonball rolling across the dim light of memory. I see her patent leather shoes, round-toed, pumping, as she chases Shadow over hills and onto someone's picnic feast, one paw deep in the center of a chocolate cake, a fried chicken leg clamped in his jaw. *He should have been on a leash!* Judy says. Their laughter pocks lilac trees that open and bloom. I'm old now; mother's my child, just like real life. Our home, many homes before, teeters, a teacup on the saucer of the lawn. Her bed, pale blue in the haze, yawns wide. *Buy me a dog*, she says, reaching for me in our long-ago kitchen.

- Because for years what lit the fuse was fury, not love.

- Because like the women in my family I have mastered putting up a front, not understanding until too late what were the wars that needed getting behind.

- Because you called me a coward. Because the truth is I was stupid, or naïve, anyway very young, sure that the loss of you was the loss of love. Because I thought loss was failure, my failure and not yours, where all I tasted smelled touched knew was what was darkest because the blame must have been mine.

- Because your ultimatum that I let anger go was more than a sprung lock, more than a breath that takes one more. Because of the fuzz on a bashful peach. Because of the stirrings inside a forest.

* * *

1. Run fast and run far.
2. Go until you reach the earth's edge.

3. There, hurl yourself off as though all about you are vistas,
   the same ones you always claimed were yours.
4. Do not imagine I am unsure about what I see, if it is fall or
   if it is flight.
5. Do not.

* * *

- Because there, on the mantelpiece, waits my loaded pistol of a
  novel.

Weeks after they moved,
    Dad went missing
        in her mind.

What does anyone know

of tangled filaments,
of clustered bits of beta-amelyoid,
of savvy caregiving,   of improvisation,

of sixty-two years of marriage,
of pints of whiskey,

of a father struggling from a floor,
a swelling bump on his head.

My ancestors are teenage girls,
they speak in sparkles and guts,
order whip cream,
kiss flowers with teeth.

They send texts that say *I never ever ever want to see you again*
cast curses with emojis,
mix acid and acronyms in a single message.

My ancestors climb trees in leggings,
nest among pine needles,
pull safety pins from their ears,
pierce robin eggs.

My ancestors wear thick eyeliner,
smudged tender like Vancouver rain,
and everyone who ever said *you'll understand when you're older.*
They pick locks to diaries,
wrap sweaters around their jeans,
when they bleed, wrap arms around each other,
screenshot the world's history and save it.

My ancestors upspeak their stories best,
creating poetry out of plastic tubes,
secrets held between glossed lips,
codes clinging to music chords.

I love my ancestors best for their loud voices,
puked stars, carbonated hearts,
memories preserved in resin and rhodium.

We don't care about your ancestors.
We don't care about your elders.

My ancestors are busy,
Archiving scraped knees, chipped acrylic nails,
the names of their best friends,
they are busy writing books,
to one day fill the greatest libraries with pink gel pens,
signatures dotted with a heart.

1. Fatigue.

Upon waking, you're ready to return to bed.
The slight pull & burn of overworked

muscles remain in your limbs all day,
a buzz like a faraway bleacherfull

of voices cheering, booing, jeering
inside your arms & legs. Your feet

are far, far; looking down your legs
at them is like gazing down a narrow,

tree-lined road at some fogged horizon.
Inaccurate fingers. Words on a page

do a shuck-jostle dance, letters
staggering over one another, drunk.

Your vision an impressionist painting.
Your vision like that in new glasses

minus the amazing every-single-leaf.
Your feet on a canted floor. You had

plans? Hopes? An itinerary? Even
a loose schedule? Ridiculous.

Thoughts unmoored, anchorless boats,
become jumbled wrack on the shore.

Your body a wet load of laundry. So
heavy. Place it on the floor. Anywhere.

2. Spiral.

Fingers pull and yearn to throw the cell
across the room, but reason forbids it.

The image of the cracked screen, the back
half popped off & skittering under sofa.

Hands also wish to shred nearest paper:
calming static of ensuing rips. You fancy

you can build a shield around the aching
organ in the chest: funny how it actually

hurts; you thought it was a metaphor.
The floor seems to hold a magnetic charge

and pulls you down, down, but this too
you Tuvok away. You build with your mind

that heart-case: a steel egg. A rounded coffin.
When it is in place the pains will be sealed in.

Sometimes in an effort to stop your thoughts
you find instead you've stilled your breathing.

3. Repetition.

You whisper in the cracks between activities at work,
It's okay. You're fine. You are going to be okay.

On the toilet, watching spirals of cat hair
tumbleweed over tiles, you say, *I want to go home.*

You spend some minutes dogging this notion, *home*,
wondering why you say it in your own house,

in your mother's house, in the car, everywhere.
What place on this side of the sod qualifies?

Is this some Biblical or metaphysical announcement:
having confessed that they are strangers and exiles

in this world? Are you longing for that *better country,*
that *Heavenly one?* You seem, then, overeager

to get there, hissing, *I am going to kill myself*
today, but you don't, & have never had, a plan.

4. Some rules.

Swear at the phone, but don't answer it. Sound
is grating so turn the TV down. If you refuse

to answer questions your mother will stop
asking them. Keep your eyes focused dead

ahead & don't move at all your neck. Soon
you won't see anything. Even the eyes

can give up, the optical center of the brain
stop collecting shapes & assigning names.

You're hungry but it's not worth walking
into the kitchen. What a master you are:

even pangs of need can be tamed. Even
the cats will nod off if you don't pet them.

5. Reasons.

You dig around in the past a bit for that
lost Easter egg that soured & has begun to stink.

It was painted a streaky pink, & found sulfurous,
cracked under the parked push mower

in the dim & grimy garage. You remember.
It was high summer, the stench demanding.

Somewhere in you you've tucked away
in folds of forgetfulness & dark grease

the seed of this thing. Was it your loved Collie,
found shot & growing formless in the forest?

An older cousin's curious hands? The wrong shoes
you wore in gradeschool, petal pink but without

the brand name, for which you were never forgiven?
The night you don't remember in high school, when you

trusted the lovely boy with the hazel eyes, foolishly?
The building gross and sticky glop of all these things,

tacky like a too-much-painted wall? Cracking
off in kaleidoscope chips when you scratch at it.

Maybe it's none of these things. You often suspect
there isn't any reason at all.

THE LENNI-LENAPE CALLED THIS GROUND IHPETONGA **KAREN NEUBERG**

From this ground, this "high, sandy bank"
I look out to the water below

still – but less so than in
Whitman's day – with ferries, barges,

tugs, leisure craft moving
between shorelines.

This tidal estuary/New York Harbor/
East River, that I view

from the end of the cul-de-sac
a few steps from my building's door,

reveals the mood of the day to me
and carries past present future

and all the intricate histories
flowing together, floating

and sinking, riding the wakes
as I, like countless others

watch the light show
sun provides on its surface.

Before I left, my doctor excised a polyp from between my legs. I thought, foolhardy still, I could return to life unscathed. How does a body hold bracing and numbness simultaneously?

When we landed in Tunis, waited for customs and the slow stamp of entry, a man spoke of his brother, *"C'était une belle mort."* It was a beautiful death. Or so I heard under the shuffle of crowds, the soft timbre of resistance to his return.

Days later, Carthage cathedral ticket agents pointed to a statue under my feet as I exited, told me in fervent French and English it was a hermaphrodite, smiled in anticipation of shock or awe, but I had seen enough ruins that day and did not raise an eyebrow, did not break my stride.

And now, I look at photos of the Borghese Hermaphrodite, re-clined in marble, soft curves inviting the hand, and wonder what I passed so quickly on my way to Punic merchant quarters and how young was I when I became hardened, fearful, questioning of the ardent calls of strange men.

She sits on the bus, the cake balanced on her knees. The carton is tied with twine, and she thinks of the cake nestled inside, perfectly decorated.

She looks at her fellow passengers. She catches the eye of the man sitting across from her and smiles at him. He nods back, and it seems to open the door to conversation, so she tells him, "It's a surprise." She taps her fingers on the box. "We've been trying for a baby …" She trails off, noticing that he has already turned away. The woman's smile falters.

They *had* been trying, her and her husband. At first it was a joke, a game they played – tracking ovulation, trying different positions. Tilting pelvis to get an assist from gravity, gagging down iron-rich smoothies, taking deep meditative breaths to keep the stress at bay. As months passed, the playfulness disappeared.

The bus pulls into the park-and-ride lot. She unlocks her car, opens the door, and waits a moment for the stale trapped heat of the day to dissipate. Then she places the cake in the back seat. She takes the turns cautiously, so the cake won't slide around and ruin the delicate decorations.

Home is a beige affair at the end of a cul-de-sac lined with similar beige neighbors. On the second floor, the nursery is already prepared. The woman had painted a mural on one wall, a spreading tree with a cartoon owl perched on a branch.

The house is quiet inside except for the gentle hum of the refrigerator. She places the cake in the kitchen and sheds her clothes, strewing them in a trail as she walks to retrieve the mail. There are credit card offers. Bills – electric, credit card, lawyer. She walks back to the kitchen.

She stands naked in the silence of the house, and the tip of her tongue worries at the corner of her mouth. There's a sore developing there, and the thin sting of pain feels good to her. She takes a knife from a drawer and saws through the twine on the cake box. She throws the lid back to reveal the cake with its elaborate frosting rosettes and smooth rolled fondant. It practically glitters with all the sugar.

She peels a strip of fondant from the cake, lays it on her tongue, and chews. It is heavy, like clay, and it leaves a film behind on her tongue as she swallows. She eats another piece and another, then the frosting rosettes with their hardened crust of sugar, until the cake is stripped nude.

She grabs a fistful of cake and buttercream. She squeezes it into a ball, then crams the whole thing in. Her jaw works through the paste of cake and frosting. The sugar burns her throat, makes her cough, forces her to slow down.

Later, she marvels at the feral quality of her hunger. She kneels in front of the toilet, delighting in how light she feels once she's purged. Her husband, in their last fight, had called her a black hole, a suck of energy and money for the things they couldn't control. Things she couldn't control.

The tiles are hard against her knees. She stands up. She looks at herself in the mirror, her sticky hands running over the rungs of her ribs. She touches her jutting hip bones and lets her hands rest on her belly, concave under her palms.

A black hole only devours, but she devours and then releases. In the releasing, she removes a bit of herself. She imagines the metals leaving her body: the calcium and potassium and magnesium. All the things that weigh her down.

Soon, all the heavy parts will be gone, and she'll be hollow-boned as a bird. She'll climb the steps up to the nursery. She'll throw open the window, and then jump, catching the updraft with her spread wings. The wind will carry her up, up. Away.

Were all painted the same flat, dead white,
were permeated with the scent of take-out containers,
had
bathtubs in the kitchen.

New York Times, New Yorkers
and *Time Out New York* lay scattered throughout
like casual love offerings.

There were
lesbian piano bars, coffee shops on corners,
absurdly lovely flower displays, Korean food
at midnight
and folded pizza slices everywhere.

A manic panoply of people thronged –
a punk rock explosion of beauty.

But I must've been a Puritan at heart –
because Emerson, Thoreau,
Dickinson and Plath
guided me back, as with a lantern,

uptown and out of the city,
hurtling on a bus back to Boston,

intimate, teacup-sized
city of my head –
as it turned out –
city of my heart.

After the painting by Edward Hopper

Tuesday matinee at the Palace on West 46th, few moviegoers dot
the house. The newsreel is over; Capra's *Lost Horizon* begins. After
guiding a latecomer to his balcony seat, an usherette idles at the
foot of the stairs, leans against the alcove wall, hourglassed with
light from a tri-shaded sconce. You may have seen her before, alone
in the *Automat* on a cold night with the same downward stare or
reading fashion magazines on the train – *Compartment C, Car 293*
– the same Ingrid Bergman hairstyle. You may be tempted to think
she's daydreaming of sunny L.A. and starring on the silver screen
opposite Ronald Coleman. But as a book opens in the film, *In
these days of wars and rumors of wars* . . . , the newsreel still flick-
ers inside her head – flimsy pacts, fascist rants, Nazi rearmament.
Flashlight under elbow, she props her chin with her hand.

WE WEREN'T TRYING TO MAKE IT SOMETHING IT NEVER WAS **EMILY WOLAHAN**

Frenzied bird song from a fern pine down the street. Shipping containers cross the Bay on business. A bare hill awaits its moment. While I don't currently have any security in this, I can say – *Look.* One mutable gaze trying to read the landscape, which I think is calm. I think the flat pale rooftops, the red peak of a tower crane, people moving cars for street sweeping, are a message. This one has notifications, has bottles hand-collected for change. While it might not be a day I can touch with triumph – still the spread of embraced water, industrial park, pine tree, the sun brief between horizon and cloud cover. A voice from behind asks me what time it is.

WHEN MY DAUGHTER TELLS ME I WAS NEVER PUNK
JESSICA WALSH

I say, honey, my being alive is punk. I made my life
out of grudges when I saw the odds placed against me,

when my role was to marry a man who'd kill me
and give me my hot young death, a guy named Charles

who would have and nearly did – the day I said *fuck you*
and threw his keys in the snow? That was punk.

When I called a nice guy who'd loved me steady
and thought *what if I can try staying alive*, that was punk;

when I had my last drink and surrendered the scene, that too was punk,
and yes I miss the me who would be dead

because I was a bottle rocket, a pipe bomb of a good time
but my being alive is the middle finger I never put down –

I did not let these days go by, I clawed each one from dirt,
and when I get my nails done I am stockpiling weapons,

when I buy groceries, when I gas up the car,
I am threatening to survive long enough to piss off

a million awful people to be alive in spite of,
I am promising to stay flagrantly alive:

This is my beautiful house. I am this beautiful wife.
How did I get here, I say, by my fucking teeth.

CAPE COD TUNDRA **KAREN POPPY**

I rise from this ocean,
Shuffle across waves
Frozen, sculpted like stone.
So cold, air terrorizes teeth.
Breath, spine white, every puff
A vertebrae, shifting bone.

Ice caps melt at each pole.
Old Silver Beach silvers over,
No tarnish before all loss of color.
Sunset whets sky sharp with invisible blaze,
With each storm-wild repetition of snow.
Other layers burn underneath.
Above, about twenty below.

Accelerated heat, slowed current.

How does it balance, how
Does it all balance out in the end?

(F)EAR - A GLIMPSE **REKHA VALLIAPPAN**

To place my ear against the ice cold window pane
hear the aged flow of dying – they wash up in
unplanned regularity on distant shores – pelicans
pipers penguins; it's a tale; it's not, mixing in odors
of sewer.

Light streams from the street through that same
window, exploring the room's insides: part of the
sign of the end
part of the sound when no birds sing; when crying
doves articulate melancholy in blips, deeper than
our own sadness

Just a year into the raging grip a monarch
butterfly can't break from its chrysalis spinning
within a mason jar; a cow's teats grow inwards; a
dream of rainforests seek frenzied seasons; torched
pine cones on a forest floor that could be your last
glimpses

In the space between your hemlock and mine many
strands break, nebulous, intense, urgent; the sky
shreds into telephone poles flipping over the icy
grey window pane double seeing the light working
up my skin: fear – to move on

Finally, the stench of the squirrel, dead behind a wall – the squirrel who used to haunt our deck, chew the wicker furniture, sploot on the railing, and hump our outdoor lights – is abating. For five weeks my husband and I have lived with windows open day and night through pollen, cold, wind, and rain. We've burned down every Yankee Candle hoarded over our thirty-five years of marriage – sometimes all at once, creating the semblance of an indoor bonfire. Now, house sealed, we await the flies.

The squirrel's demise coincides with the waning of the pandemic. Vaccinated after a long and challenging year, Steve and I are ready to broaden our in-person social lives, so we invite friends and family to stop by. However, the stench keeps all visiting outside.

We believe the squirrel was displaced when our neighbors stripped their yard of some trees. A huge mobile crane, Iron Tree, rumbled in two months ago and expelled men, quick and light as squirrels, to shimmy up each towering tree, and yoke its neck. Then Iron Tree lifted them, one at a time, like a mother cat a kitten, up and over another neighbor's house and into a chipper we heard but could not see.

The squirrel must have been looking for a new place to nest when it tumbled down a chute and into our home's innards. Poor thing. In truth, I loathed him, so I'm surprised at the pity I feel. He must have been scared, thirsty and hungry, lost inside a maze of joists and jutting nails. He died before we could trap him and set him free. Thus the pity – but also hope – hoping against hope he wasn't a she who'd left a litter.

Anyway, we try not to obsess. We're vaccinated! We can leave! So when I can't take it anymore, I drive to Gloucester to swim and walk and take underwater photographs with my sister and her wife. Their puppy, Pinky, comes along. We walk two miles through woods to reach a pond – a closely held secret place – where there's a small beach. We shimmy into wetsuits and plunge.

While my sister-in-law searches out driftwood and good spots for taking photographs, my sister and I swim across. We pause in the middle of the pond, float on our backs, and note our gratitude to our long-gone parents for teaching us to swim, for kindling our love of sky and water. A landlubber, Pinky stares us down, whimpering from the shore.

When we reach the opposite bank, we get out and my sister leads me across a spit of land to an adjoining pond. We happen upon a couple of naked sunbathers, and she and I gape like we're from outer space all sealed up in our wetsuits, hats, gloves and booties. Sun-drunk and sluggish, the sunbathers note us with a smile and a wave before we turn discreetly away, and plunge back to return, Neoprene muskrats, the way we came.

the details have been removed. Cardinal song
is now every bird's song. People's faces
smoothed as if by a lathe. The sun just a child's
yellow circle with those rays jutting out.

I've had some time to think about the minds
of children. I'm already past that myself.
Then I crack the shell of the hard-boiled egg,
eat with the tongue and nose of a 10 year old.

Smell the canned sweetness of the tomato
soup I make for my girl. I remember how I'd melt
a pat of butter over the top, the fat slicking out
over the skin of the surface, the ghee separating,

though I didn't have a name for it then. They've
become addicted. Hasn't everyone? Humans
are addicts and there's nothing that can be done.
Addiction feels like the groove in a scratched record,

the scab that heals over a wound
only to be picked off again. That smoke
that rakes over the coals of your throat
outside, with snow on the ground, sick with fever,

getting your fix before your parents come home.
Pregnancy is what stopped my habit. Maybe
the kids just need to grow up. They are still
adding details, subtracting them. What used to feel

like a gift becomes hard work and practice. The sketch
you make at 5, 16, and 50. Your thigh
and how it's changed. Your stomach.
Whose hand is placed lovingly there.

Instead of filing down their brains to numbness,
they find the network of stars as if it were their own
synapses on fire. Venture out into the woods
when it snows, just to feel their face wet with something

other than tears. To love what they've reclaimed
because they cared for themselves for once. *Pentimento*,
a word I just learned, Italian for "repentance",
a visible trace of earlier painting beneath layers of paint.

No, not erasure, after which the paper feels rough,
scoured. The scatterings brushed away with the side of a hand.

SWITCHING LANES **CHARLES BRICE**

On that clear Thanksgiving Day
       our old van changed lanes
smooth as a red-tailed hawk
       rides thermals. I was headed towards
my brother-in-law's home in D.C.
       where turkey, dressing, sweet-potatoes,
and suspended resentments
       awaited our arrival.

Safely ensconced in the middle lane
       of I-95, sure that I was headed
in the right direction, I began to think
       of my parents' friend Barry,
the night he reached into my pajamas
       and fondled my penis
while I slept with him during his visit
       to our home in 1955
when I was five years old.

I'd asked if I could sleep with him
            in the way I might sleep
with a favorite toy or pet. That night
            he shoved his hand into my pajamas
and whispered, "Betty." When I told my mother,
            she laughed. "He must have
been missing his wife," she chortled,
            and laughed some more.

All those years I'd associated that memory only
            with my mother's laughter. But
on that pristine fall day, when
            our old van switched lanes
like an eagle swoops down and
            carries away a salmon,
I understood.

SPHERES AND INFLUENCES **MARY ANN DIMAND**

– For Ny and Francesca

The smell of smoke
at night is no oracle
of grilled meats now. The mountains,
afire. The plague, red
hot, and people maddened to flame, to gasoline
themselves or neighbors, strike
a match. We're burning
our bridges and calling it thrift. It's raw
down here, and cinder-scourged.
The lower sky is clogged
with ash and shouting. I look up,
up past the looming ghosts
of muffled mountains, up
to thinner air, darkened
by the universe beyond it.
There's space behind the sky.
It's very cold, and full of distances
and bigger forges. But as I pause

between the chill and conflagration, I track
the wave of Neowise greeting
our grim planet, and the wink
of fireflies, sentinels of grass
and roof-edge. We are embedded
in a world of allies. Bright bees
and subtle worms, the beetles
that tote the dung and tend
the corpses, plankton twinkling from the seas,
redwoods ever reaching and creaking, whales
with their long slow songs. We
none of us leave this globe
unchanged, none have no impact, none
can say "Myself alone" and have it
mean something. Let our breath
be sweet; our steps leave mossy
paths to where we'd want to gather.

"The Antarctic cold definitely feels a lot different from the cold in Idaho," Adam said.

"Sure does," Rodger said as he flicked the mini-icicles off of his thick mustache. "Once we cross this next glacier wall, we'll have reached the edge of the earth."

Adam and Rodger trudged on with their overstuffed backpacks through the wintry terrain, looking like a pair of snails with shells full of climbing equipment and survival supplies.

"I really think we should turn around," Adam said.

"But we're almost there," Rodger said.

Rodger pulled out his map. A harsh gust of wind swept it off into the snowy distance.

"See!" Adam said. "Even the wind is telling us to go back!"

Rodger checked his compass. The red needle was frozen stiff, as if it had given up on doing its one and only job. Rodger tapped the glass face of the compass, but the needle wouldn't budge.

"It's so cold that the compass broke," Adam said. "If that isn't a sign, I don't know what is."

"It's not broken," Rodger said. "It's just confused."

Adam sighed and rolled his eyes. "How much further do we have to go?"

Rodger pointed ahead with the focus of an olympic athlete. "If we keep moving, we should get to the glacier wall within an hour," he said.

Adam came to a halt and forcefully planted his boots into the snow. "I have something to tell you," he said.

"What?" Rodger asked as he hiked on.

"I don't really think the earth is flat," Adam answered.

Rodger choked on his own snot from laughing so hard. "You're kidding," he said.

"Rodger!" Adam said. "It just doesn't make sense!"

Rodger stopped. "Wait," he said. "You're being serious?"

"Yes!" Adam answered.

"Did you not watch the YouTube documentary I sent you?" Rodger asked.

"No one ever actually watches videos that people send them," Adam said. "Especially when they're two-hours-long."

"Then why did you decide to come?" Rodger asked.

Adam took a deep breath. "I thought it would be a good bonding experience."

Rodger squints. "A bonding experience?"

"I just feel like we've been drifting apart from each other the past few years," Adam said. "Like, there's this fracture growing between us."

Rodger took a seat in the snow. "I've always wanted to accomplish something amazing before I turn thirty," he said. "You know, to prove that there's something special about me."

"Please don't go all Marlon Brando in On the Waterfront on me," Adam said.

"It's true," Rodger said. "I feel like my life has been disappointment after disappointment."

"You've been my best and only friend for almost my whole life," Adam said. "That's a pretty awesome accomplishment."

Rodger entered a deep stare. "I'd shed a tear right now but it might freeze," he said.

Adam smiled. "Let's go," he said as he held his hand out to Rodger. "Let's get to that glacier wall."

Rodger grabbed Adam's hand and popped up from the ground. "To the glacier wall!"

Adam dusted the snow off of his coat. "After that, I'm not going any further."

"There is no further," Rodger answered.

Sam Ambler has published in *Christopher Street*, *The James White Review, and City Lights Review* Number 2, among others. He won the San Francisco Bay Guardian's 6th Annual Poetry Contest. He has a BA in English, specializing in creative writing of poetry, from Stanford University.

Catherine Arra is the author of *Her Landscape, Poems Based on the Life of Mileva Marić Einstein* (Finishing Line Press, 2020), *(Women in Parentheses)* (Kelsay Books, 2019), *Writing in the Ether* (Dos Madres Press, 2018), and three chapbooks. She lives in the Hudson Valley in upstate New York. Find her at www.catherinearra.com.

Tina Barry is the author of *Beautiful Raft*, and *Mall Flower.* Her writing can be found in *Best Small Fictions 2020* (spotlighted story) and *2016*, *Drunken Boat, Inch Magazine, Nasty Women Poets, A Constellation of Kisses* and elsewhere.

Lynn Bey has published short stories and flash fiction published in *The Literarian* (nominated for a Pushcart award), *New World Writing, The Binnacle* (nominated for a Pushcart award and joint winner of the Eleventh Annual Ultra-Short Competition), *Digital Americana, Scribble Magazine, The Brooklyner, Birmingham Arts Journal*, and other magazines.

Heather Bourbeau has published in *100 Word Story, Alaska Quarterly Review, The MacGuffin, Meridian, The Stockholm Review of Literature*, and *SWWIM*. She has twice been nominated for a Pushcart Prize. She has worked with various UN agencies, including the UN peacekeeping mission in Liberia and UNICEF Somalia.

Christine Boyer has been published in *The Little Patuxent Review*, *The Tahoma Literary Review*, and *So It Goes:* the Literary Journal of the Kurt Vonnegut Museum and Library, among others. She is a student with Harvard University Extension School and lives in Massachusetts.
Her website is www.christine-boyer.com.

Charles Brice won the 2020 Field Guide Magazine Poetry Contest. His chapbook, *All the Songs Sung* (Angel Flight Press), and his fourth poetry collection, *The Broad Grin of Eternity* (WordTech Editions) arrived in 2021. His poetry has been nominated for the Best of Net Anthology and three times for a Pushcart Prize.

Aaron Caycedo-Kimura is author of *Ubasute* (Slapering Hol Press, 2021) and the forthcoming *Common Grace* (Beacon Press, 2022). He is a recipient of a Robert Pinsky Global Fellowship and a St. Botolph Club Foundation Emerging Artist Award. His work appears in *Beloit Poetry Journal*, *Poet Lore*, *DMQ Review*, and elsewhere.

Eileen Cleary earned MFA's at Lesley University and Solstice. She's a Pushcart nominee and has published in *Naugatuck River Review*, *J Journal*, *The American Journal of Poetry* and *Main Street Rag*. She has published two books, *Child Ward of the Commonwealth* (Main Street Rag Press, 2019), and *2 a.m. with Keats* (Nixes Mate Books, 2020).

Mary Ann Dimand lives with One husband, one son, two cats, and many outgrown hockey sticks. She is busy converting a small horse property to a small farm.

Frances Donovan has published in *The Rumpus*, *Heavy Feather Review*, *SWWIM*, *Solstice*, and elsewhere. Her chapbook *Mad Quick Hand of the Sea-*

shore was a finalist in the Lambda Literary Awards. She holds an MFA in poetry from Lesley University and once drove a bulldozer in an LGBTQ+ Pride Parade. gardenofwords.com. Twitter: @okelle.

Jennifer Franklin has published two full-length poetry collections, most recently *No Small Gift* (Four Way Books, 2018). Her third book, *If Some God Shakes Your House*, will be published by Four Way Books in 2023. Her work has been published or is forthcoming in *American Poetry Review, Boston Review, Gettysburg Review, Guernica, JAMA, Los Angeles Review, The Nation, New England Review, Paris Review, Plume,* "poem-a-day" on poets.org, and *Prairie Schooner.* She lives in New York City. Her website is jenniferfranklinpoet.com.

Karen Friedland is a grant writer by day who has published in *The Lily Poetry Review, Writing in a Women's Voice, Vox Populi* and others. One of her poems was nominated for a Pushcart Prize and another was displayed on the walls of Boston's City Hall. Her books of poems are *Tales from the Teacup Palace* (Červená Barva Press) and *Places That Are Gone* (Nixes Mate Books).

Mary Beth Hines writes poetry, short fiction and non-fiction from her home in Massachusetts. Her prose and poetry has appeared in journals such as *Literary Mama, Madcap Review, Ruminate, Crab Orchard Review, Eclectica, Nixes Mate Review,* and *SWWIM* among others.

Mary Honaker is the author of *Becoming Persephone* (Third Lung Press, 2019) and the chapbooks *It Will Happen Like This* (YesNo Press, 2015) and *Gwen and the Big Nothing* (The Orchard Street Press, 2020.) She holds an MFA from Lesley University. She lives in Beaver, West Virginia.

Amanda Hope lives in eastern Massachusetts with her partner and cats. A graduate of Colgate University and Simmons College, she works as a librarian. Her chapbook, *The Museum of Resentments*, was published by Paper Nautilus in 2020. You can find her on Twitter at @AmandaHopePoet.

Carrie Jewell has been teaching high school English for 18 years. Her poems have appeared in *The Worcester Review* and *What Rough Beast*. She is a mother of two, an Outward Bound alum, an amateur gardener, and an avid Ferrante fan.

Christine Jones is founder/editor-in-chief of Poems2go and an associate editor of *Lily Poetry Review*. Her poems have appeared in *32 poems, cagibi, Sugar House Review, Mom Egg Review, SWWIM, Pangyrus, Salamander, Solstice, Passengers Journal*, and elsewhere. She is the author of, *Girl Without a Shirt* (Finishing Line Press, 2020) and co-editor of the recently released anthology, *Voices Amidst the Virus: Poets Respond to the Pandemic* (Lily Poetry Review Books, 2020).

Crystal Karlberg is a poet and library assistant at her local library. Her work has been published by *Oddball Magazine, Rust & Moth, Psaltery and Lyre*, and *The Museum of Americana*. Her poem "Dream in Blue" was nominated for a Pushcart Prize.

Sharon Kennedy-Nolle is a graduate of Vassar College, with an MFA and doctoral degree from the University of Iowa. A participant in the Bread Loaf Conferences in both Middlebury and Sicily in 2016, she was also accepted to the Sewanee Writers' Conference in 2018.

Linda Lamenza is a poet and literacy specialist in Massachusetts. Her work is forthcoming or has appeared in *Constellations, Rogue Agent, Main Street Rag,*

The Comstock Review, *The Tishman Review*, and elsewhere. She is a member of Poemworks: The Workshop for Publishing Poets. Linda is fluent in Italian and enjoys spending time at the beach reading and writing.

Yvonne Higgins Leach spent decades balancing a career in communications and public relations, raising a family, and pursuing her love of writing poetry. She is the author of *Another Autumn* (Cherry Grove Collections, *2014*). Her latest passion is working with shelter dogs. She splits her time living in Vashon and Spokane, Washington. yvonnehigginsleach.com

Kasy Long is an Indiana-based freelance writer and editor. She serves as the Editor-in-Chief of *Remington Review*. Her work has previously been published in *Constellate Literary Journal, Inside the Bell Jar, Glass Mountain, Oracle Fine Arts Review, The Sigma Tau Delta Rectangle*, and elsewhere.

Colleen Michaels hosts The Improbable Places Poetry Tour bringing poetry to unlikely places like tattoo parlors, laundromats, and swimming pools. Her poems have appeared in journals and anthologies including *Barrelhouse, The Paterson Literary Review, Mom Egg Review* and *Raising Lilly Ledbetter: Women Poets Occupy the Workspace* (Lost Horse Press). Her poems have been commissioned as installations by The Massachusetts Poetry Festival, The Peabody Essex Museum, and The Trustees of Reservations.

Zach Murphy is a Hawaii-born writer with a background in cinema. His stories appear in *Reed Magazine, Ginosko Literary Journal, The Coachella Review, Mystery Tribune, Ruminate, Sheepshead Review, Wilderness House Literary Review*, and *Flash: The International Short-Short Story Magazine*. His debut chapbook

Tiny Universes is available via Selcouth Station Press. He lives with his wonderful wife Kelly in St. Paul, Minnesota.

Karen Neuberg is a Brooklyn, NY,-based poet. Her poems have appeared or are forthcoming in *Black Moon, Gone Lawn, Inflectionist Review, Muddy River Review*, and *Verse Daily.* She is the author of the full-length poetry collection, *Pursuit* (Kelsay Press, *2019)* and the chapbook *The Elephants are Asking* (Glass Lyre, 2017) She holds an MFA from the New School and is associate editor of the online poetry journal *First Literary Review-East.*

Jonathan Penton founded UnlikelyStories.org in 1998, and has run it as a journal of literature, art, and sociopolitical content since. He expanded with Unlikely Books in 2005. He has provided technical and management expertise to arts organizations including the New Orleans Poetry Festival, MadHat, Inc., and Big Bridge.

Kenneth Pobo has a new book out from Circling Rivers called *Loplop in a Red City.* His work has appeared in: *Mudfish, Nimrod, Hawaii Review, Bay Windows*, and elsewhere.

Karen Poppy has published in numerous literary journals, magazines, and anthologies. She has published two chapbooks, *Crack Open/Emergency* (Finishing Line Press, 2020), and *Every Possible Thing* (Homestead Lighthouse Press, 2020). Her latest chapbook, *Our Own Beautiful Brutality* was published in 2021 with Finishing Line Press. karenpoppy.com

Jessica Purdy teaches Poetry Workshops at Southern New Hampshire University. Her poems and reviews have appeared in *Gargoyle, The Plath Poetry Project,*

The Ekphrastic Review, Nixes Mate Review, Bluestem, and *The Cafe Review*, among others. She has published one chapbook, *Learning the Names*, (Finishing Line Press, 2015), and two books *STARLAND* and *Sleep in a Strange House* (both Nixes Mate Books, consecutively, in 2017 and 2018).

KI RUSSELL is author of the hybrid genre novel *The Wolf at the Door* (Ars Omnia Publishing, 2014), the poetry collection *Antler Woman Responds* (Paladin Contemporaries, 2014) and the chapbook *How to Become Baba Yaga* (Medulla Publishing, 2011). She is a peer reviewer for the online literary journal *Whale Road Review*. She teaches writing and literature at Blue Mountain Community College.

ARIANNA SEBO is a queer poet and writer living in Southern Alberta with her husband, pug, and five cats. Follow her at AriannaSebo.com and @AriannaSebo on Twitter and Instagram.

MARGARITA SERAFIMOVA is the winner of the 2020 biennial Tony Quagliano/ Hawai'i Council for the Humanities International Award. She has a chapbook, *A Surgery of A Star*. Her digital chapbook, *'En-tîm' ('Forest')*, is forthcoming by the San Francisco State University Poetry Center in 2021. Her work appears widely, including at *Nixes Mate, Nashville Review, LIT, Agenda Poetry, Poetry South, Botticelli, Shrew, Steam Ticket, Waxwing, A-Minor, Trafika Europe, Noble/ Gas, Obra/ Artifact, Great Weather for Media*, and *Landfill*.

BEATE SIGRIDDAUGHTER grew up in Nürnberg, Germany. Her playgrounds were a nearby castle and World War II bomb ruins. She lives in Silver City, New Mexico, where she was poet laureate from 2017 to 2019. In her blog *Writing In A Woman's Voice*, she publishes other women's work. Follow her at sigriddaughter.net.

Sarah Dickenson Snyder has written poetry since she knew there was a form of writing with conscious linebreaks. She has three poetry collections: *The Human Contract* (2017), *Notes from a Nomad* (nominated for the Massachusetts Book Awards 2018), and *With a Polaroid Camera* (2019). Recently, poems have appeared in *Rattle*, *Artemis*, *The Sewanee Review*, and *RHINO*.

Susan Tepper is the author of eight published books of fiction and poetry. She has received eighteen Pushcart Prize Nominations, a Pulitzer Prize Nomination for the epistolary novel *What May Have Been* (Červená Barva Press 2010, currently being adapted as a stage play), Best Story of *17 Years of Vestal Review*, and other honors. Tepper's new book is a zany road novel titled *What Drives Men*. susantepper.com.

Gail Thomas has two collections of poems with Four Way Books: *Inscriptions* (2014), and *Cathedral of Wish* (2006), winner of the Norma Farber First Book Award. Her poems are forthcoming or have recently appeared in *Tampa Review*, *Ocean State Review*, *The Missouri Review* and elsewhere. Cammy lives in Lexington, Massachusetts.

Meg Tuite is author of a novel-in-stories, *Domestic Apparition*, a short story collection, *Bound By Blue*, and won the Twin Antlers Collaborative Poetry award for her poetry collection, *Bare Bulbs Swinging*, as well as five chapbooks of short fiction, flash, and poetic prose. She teaches at Santa Fe Community College, is a senior editor at Connotation Press and *(b)OINK* lit zine, and editor of nine anthologies. megtuite.com

Rekha Valliappan is a writer of prose and poetry published in *Ann Arbor Review, the Sandy River Review, The Pangolin Review, Wilderness House Literary Review, Wellington Street Review, The London Reader, Red Fez, Prime Number Magazine / Press 53*, and elsewhere. Her poem was nominated for the Pushcart Prize by *Liquid Imagination*.

Jessica Walsh is the author of two poetry collections and two chapbooks. Her work has appeared in *Lunch Ticket, RHINO, Tinderbox, Whale Road Review, Fatal Flaw Lit*, and more. A native of rural Michigan, she now lives and teaches in the Chicago suburbs. jessicalwalsh.com

Emily Wolahan is the author of the poetry collection *Hinge* (NPRP, 2015). Her poetry has appeared in *Puerto del Sol, Sixth Finch, Georgia Review*, and *Oversound*. She is currently pursuing a Ph.D. in Anthropology and Social Change (CIIS) and is a Poetry Editor at *Tinderbox Poetry Journal*.

Hannah Yerington is a Jewish Arts educator, and the director of the Bolinas Poetry Camp for Girls. Her work has been published in *Rogue Agent, River Heron Review*, and the *Racket*, among others. She is currently an MFA candidate at Bowling Green State University.

42° 19' 47.9" N 70° 56' 43.9" W

Nixes Mate is a navigational hazard in Boston Harbor used during the colonial period to gibbet and hang pirates and mutineers.

Nixes Mate Books features small-batch artisanal literature, created by writers who use all 26 letters of the alphabet and then some, honing their craft the time-honored way: one line at a time.

nixesmate.pub

www.ingramcontent.com/pod-product-compliance
Lightning Source LLC
Chambersburg PA
CBHW080520030726
47592CB00012B/3412